D1515901

PICTURE READING STORIES

Learning to read requires many more skills than just decoding words. This lively, colourful book is based on children's experiences and on fictional stories.

It is designed for young children who are not yet reading and for many who have already begun. It will encourage them to look closely at pictures, to spot similarities and differences, to practise sequencing and anticipation, and to enjoy using imagination and language while 'reading' the stories told in pictures.

On each double page, the artist has hidden a little ladybird like this:

Can your child find it?

British Library Cataloguing in Publication Data

Haselden, Mary
　　Picture-reading stories.
　　I. Title　　II. Sliwinska, Sara　　III. Series
　　823'.914[J]
　　ISBN 0-7214-1204-1

First edition

Published by Ladybird Books Ltd Loughborough Leicestershire UK
Ladybird Books Inc Auburn Maine 04210 USA
© LADYBIRD BOOKS LTD MCMXC

Printed in England

picture reading stories

99747

by MARY HASELDEN
illustrated by SARA SLIWINSKA

Ladybird Books

Find **one** difference
in each pair of pictures.

There are **six** differences
in the bottom picture.

Happy birthday!
Tell the story.

Oh dear!
What has happened?

A walk round a zoo

Follow the numbers and keep to the path.

Which animals do you see?

New babies

What is happening in the pictures?

Have you seen a new baby?

Have you been to these places?

Which did you like best?

Going to school

*Talk about the pictures
and tell the story.*

How might each story end?

Which do you think comes *first* in each row?

Lost in the supermarket

Tell the story.

Have you ever been lost?

What did **you** do?

What would you like to happen in the *middle* of each story?

*Choose a picture from this page which **you** think tells the best story.*

Tell this story

Can you see someone who doesn't belong in the story?

Tell the story

Put the pictures in the right order.

There is a clue in each picture to help you.

Going out for the day

You choose how you go and where you go.

You can tell lots of different stories.